EASTER, HERE I COME!

To my creative wings, Jane and Anu—DJS

To my biggest inspirations: Aryati, Julie, and Levin—EW

GROSSET & DUNLAP
An Imprint of Penguin Random House LLC, New York

Text copyright © 2021 by David Steinberg. Illustrations copyright © 2021 by Emanuel Wiemans.
All rights reserved. Published by Grosset & Dunlap, an imprint of Penguin Random House LLC, New York.
GROSSET & DUNLAP is a registered trademark of Penguin Random House LLC.
Manufactured in China.

Visit us online at www.penguinrandomhouse.com.

Library of Congress Control Number: 2020031778

ISBN 9780593224014   10 9 8 7 6 5 4 3 2 1

EASTER, HERE I COME!

BY D. J. STEINBERG

ILLUSTRATED BY EMANUEL WIEMANS

GROSSET & DUNLAP

SPRING FLING

Buttercups and bumblebees,
squirrels racing through the trees,
spiders sailing in on strings,
hummingbirds on humming wings,

ladybugs and butterflies,
picnic blankets, berry pies,
children going for a swing—
everybody's out for **spring!**

FUNNY BUNNY EARS

My sister loves her bunny ears.
She made them from paper and glue.
She keeps them on her head all day
and sleeps with them on, too!

MY CHOCOLATE BUNNY

Hello there, Chocolate Bunny.
It's very nice to meet you.
And now, if you don't mind,
I think I'm going to eat you!

BOB'S LITTLE SECRET

This is Bob, our classroom rabbit,
and I know it may sound funny,
but secretly, I think that Bob's
the *real-life* Easter Bunny.

On Easter, he slips from his cage
and sneaks his way outside,
then *hippity-hops* all over town
with Easter eggs to hide.

9

And when he's done, *lickety-split*,
he sneaks back without a peep,
so when we show up Monday,
Bob's back in his cage, asleep!

THE BUNNY BOP

Want to do the Bunny Bop?
All you do is hop-hop-hop.
Forward, backward—flop your ears.
Left, right—shake your bunny rears.
Keep on hopping. Never stop
until you hop in bed—*ker-PLOP!*

HOW TO DYE AN EGG
(IN ONE EASY-PEASY LESSON)

Drip 20 drops of color
in one warm-water bowl.
Add a spoon of vinegar
and a boiled egg whole.
Dunk it for 5 minutes,
remove it and air-dry it,
and, look, I dyed an egg!
Easy-peasy! Want to try it?

WHAT A SIGHT!

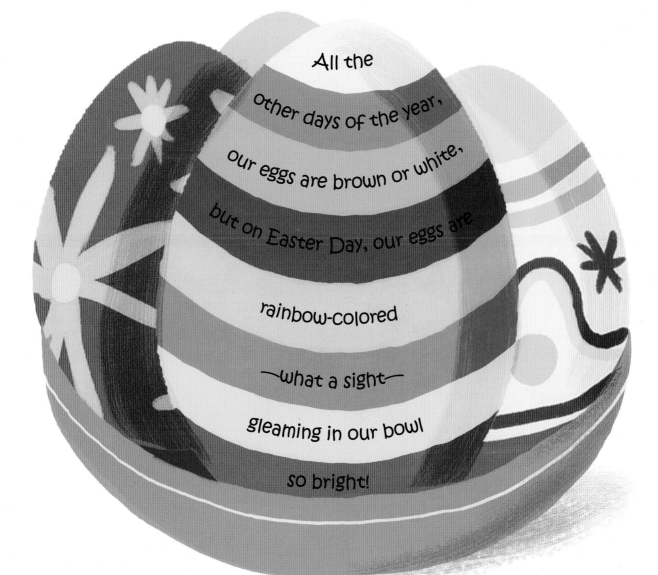

All the

other days of the year,

our eggs are brown or white,

but on Easter Day, our eggs are

rainbow-colored

—what a sight—

gleaming in our bowl

so bright!

UH-OH!

We colored all the Easter eggs,
just the way we planned.
But that's not *all* I colored . . .
Uh-oh! Look at my hand!

CR-R-RACK!

My Easter egg sprouted a crack.
There's no way to uncrack it back!
So . . . I'll peel off its shell,
salt and pepper it well,
and—*voilà*—a hard-boiled egg snack!

THE EASTER HUNTERS

We are the Easter Hunters.
It's Easter eggs we seek.
'Cross land and sea and jungle,
the Easter Hunters sneak.

We peek inside the bushes
and underneath the slide.
If *you* were an Easter egg,
where would you like to hide?

CAN YOU FIND TEN EGGS?

Now when we're all done hunting,
I count up all my eggs,
and plop down on the grass
to rest my tired hunter legs!

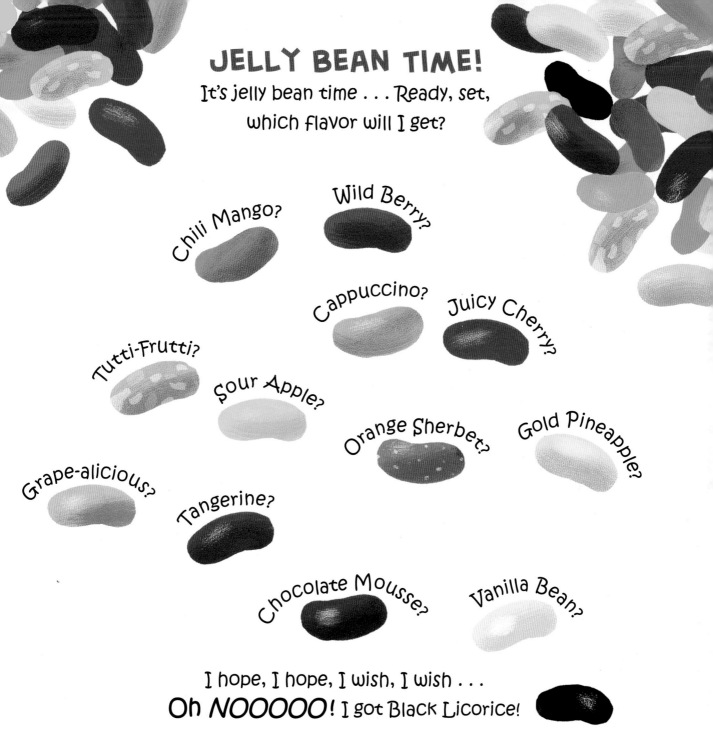

JELLY BEAN TIME!

It's jelly bean time . . . Ready, set,
which flavor will I get?

Chili Mango?

Wild Berry?

Cappuccino?

Juicy Cherry?

Tutti-Frutti?

Sour Apple?

Orange Sherbet?

Gold Pineapple?

Grape-alicious?

Tangerine?

Chocolate Mousse?

Vanilla Bean?

I hope, I hope, I wish, I wish . . .
Oh *NOOOOO*! I got Black Licorice!

A GIFT FOR GRANDMA

I picked some wildflowers
I saw along the way.
I gave them to my grandma,
who said I made her day!

She put them in a fancy vase
on top of her buffet
and made sure everyone who came
admired her bouquet!

BONNETS

So many bonnets. Which one will it be?
I have to find one that is perfect for *me*!

Too frilly

Too silly

Too floppy

Too tight

Too poofy

Too goofy

Too expensive . . .

just right!

MY BROTHER CAN'T JUGGLE

My brother can't juggle.
He thinks that he can.
He should *not* juggle eggs.
Do not try it—*oh man!*
Up they go.
(He does have that *UP* part down pat.)
Down they come.
(It's that *down* part . . .)
Look out—

SPLAT!

SPLAT!

SPLAT!

EASTER BEST

We wake up Easter morning
to get all Easter-dressed.
I wear my brand-new bow tie
and my spiffy hat and vest.

26

My sisters look all flouncy.
Mom and Dad look clean and pressed.
We head to church to see our friends
all in their Easter best!

OUR EGG-CELLENT EASTER BRUNCH

It's not *EGG*-xactly breakfast
and it's not *EGG*-xactly lunch,
but it's *EGG*-xactly in between—
our *EGG*-cellent Easter brunch.

Three guesses what we're serving!
Did you say *eggs*? You are corr-*EGG*-t!
Hey, it's our *EGG*-cellent Easter brunch—
what else did you *EGG*-spect?!

THE GREAT EGG ROLL OF 1878

Long ago, 'round Easter time, in 1878,
a bunch of kids came knocking at the White House gate.
They asked, "Can we play here on the president's lawn?"
Rutherford B. Hayes said, "I'm the president—come on!"

The children all brought eggs for an Egg Roll race
and rolled them with their spoons all over the place.
Rutherford B. Hayes said, "Come back now, y'hear?"
and sure enough they did—the very next year.

And that's why every Easter, ever since those days,
there's an Egg Roll at the White House, thanks to Rutherford B. Hayes!